INVESTIGATING GHOSTS IN HOUSES

Matilda Snowden

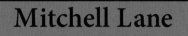

PUBLISHERS

mitchelllane.com

2001 SW 31st Avenue
Hallandale, FL 33009

First Edition, 2021.
Author: Matilda Snowden
Designer: Ed Morgan
Editor: Joyce Markovics

Series: Investigating Ghosts!
Title: Investigating Ghosts in Houses / by Matilda Snowden

Hallandale, FL : Mitchell Lane Publishers, [2021]

Library bound ISBN: 978-1-68020-635-7
eBook ISBN: 978-1-68020-636-4

CONTENTS

Words in **bold** can be found in the Glossary.

HAUNTED HOUSES

On a dead-end street sits a crumbling house wrapped in ivy. Inside, a **paranormal** investigator looks around with a flashlight. On the walls, torn wallpaper resembles peeling skin. As she walks, dust rises into the air like puffs of smoke. All of a sudden, the tiny hairs on the ghost hunter's neck stand up. She hears the distinct sound of long fingernails slowly

scraping against a wall. She follows the sound to a corner and shines her light. Before her very eyes, the wallpaper starts pulsing. It then appears to move as if a person's hand is reaching behind it! Terrified, the ghost hunter runs for the door . . . only to find that it's locked.

Across the United States are houses that are believed to be haunted. People report strange smells, sounds, or unexplainable cold areas in these spooky homes. Sometimes, alarming apparitions appear in rooms or stairways. What explains this ghostly activity? Do the spirits of the dead really dwell in these houses? There is a devoted group who want to find out. These ghost hunters, also known as paranormal investigators, gather evidence to prove that ghosts are real.

Turn the page to read startling stories about reportedly haunted houses. And follow teams of paranormal investigators who seek to uncover the truth about ghosts.

INTERESTING FACT
. . . .

VILLISCA AXE MURDER HOUSE

Villisca, Iowa

On the morning of June 11, 1912, the J. B. Moore family home was still and quiet. Neighbor Mary Peckham thought this was strange since the house was always stirring with activity. She knocked on the door. No one answered. Alarmed, she contacted J. B.'s brother Ross. "Something terrible has happened here," Ross said soon after arriving at the Moore house. Inside, he made a grisly discovery. He found the bloody bodies of his brother, sister-in-law, their four children, and two young guests.

All eight people had been hacked to death with an axe. Who was responsible for such a horrible and shocking crime?

INTERESTING FACT

Villisca is a small farming town in southern Iowa. The Moore family was well liked in the community.

After the murders, police searched for evidence left by the killer but found little. No one was ever charged with the crime. To this day, the case remains unsolved. Since the killings, the Villisca house is said to be a hive of paranormal activity. People who have stayed in the home reported hearing crying, footsteps, and the sound of dripping blood. They have also seen terrifying things that they can't explain.

Around 2010, paranormal investigators Zak Bagans and Nick Groff and their team spent a night in the Villisca house. They locked themselves inside so that no one could disturb their investigation. Zak and Nick brought a lot of equipment to help them find any evidence of ghosts. These tools included digital recorders, thermal imaging tools, and various meters.

J. W. Moore, wife and 3 of 4 children who were murdered in bed at Villisca, Ia. Star shows room in which Misses Stillinger, visiting Moores, were killed.

During the last two years, a madman murderer has killed four whole families in the West. In each case he used an axe. The murders have been at Colorado Springs, Ellsworth, Kan., Guilford, Mo., and Villisca, Ia. The last, that of the Moores at Villisca, occurred this week. The slayer shows a terrible ingenuity in making good his escape. Villisca police arrested Sam Moyer, relative of Moore family. Produced alibi. Released.

———o—o———

Irishman: "Give me three cigars."	Irishman: "Give me the strong ones. The weak ones break in
Shopman: "Strong or mild?"	my pocket!"

A newspaper article from June 14, 1912, about the Villisca murders

INTERESTING FACT

In 1930, Bonnie and Homer Ritter lived in the Villisca Axe Murder House. Bonnie often woke up at night to the sight of a man holding an axe at the foot of her bed. And Homer repeatedly heard footsteps on the stairs.

Zak and Nick set up a night-vision camera in one of the hallways. To their surprise, it recorded the sound of footsteps—and then a door slamming on its own! Zak thought a noisy ghost called a poltergeist had forcefully pushed the door shut. Or was it the killer's spirit?

Zak and his team also used special digital audio recorders in hopes of recording an EVP, or "electronic voice phenomena." Ghost hunters believe that EVPs can capture the voices and sounds of the dead. One of the clearest EVPs that Zak's crew got was a man's voice that seemed to say, "I . . . killed . . . six kids." Does the recording prove that the murderer was in the house—and speaking from beyond the grave?

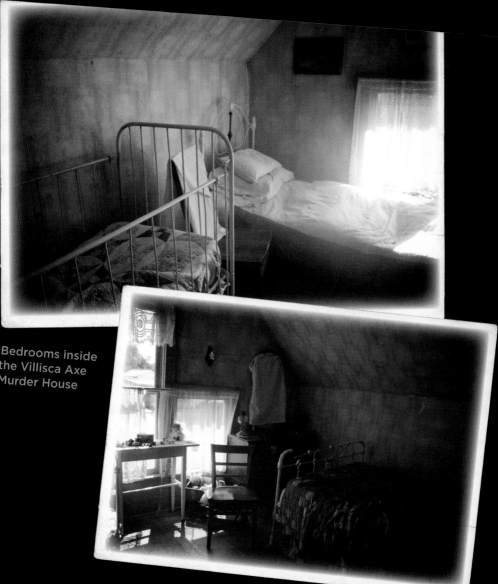

Bedrooms inside the Villisca Axe Murder House

INTERESTING FACT

Other paranormal investigators have visited the Villisca Axe Murder House. While inside, one ghost hunter felt the breath knocked out of him. He later found deep scratches on his back. He believes a ghost attacked him.

Winchester Mystery House

San Jose, California

The Winchester Mystery House is one of the strangest and, some say, most haunted places in the country. It was the home of Sarah Winchester, **heiress** to the Winchester rifle fortune. Sarah's first and only child died soon after birth. Then her husband passed away in 1881. Overcome with sadness, Sarah met with a **medium**, hoping to contact her dead loved ones.

The Winchester Mystery House

Sarah Winchester

The medium told her that her family was cursed because of all the people who had been killed by Winchester rifles. In order to fight the curse, the medium instructed Sarah to build a home for the spirits. According to the medium, as long as Sarah kept building the house, she would remain alive. But if she stopped, she too would die.

INTERESTING FACT

After Sarah's husband died, she inherited over $20 million dollars. Eventually, she would use much of that money to build her "spirit house."

Sarah began building the house in 1884. She hired carpenters to work around the clock. Nearly 40 years later, the house was still under construction. In the end, the mansion was a maze of 160 rooms, 47 fireplaces, 40 staircases, and 6 kitchens. Stranger still, the house had doors that opened onto walls, trapdoors, and a staircase that led nowhere. Sarah also built a special room to **commune** with the spirits that she believed lived alongside her in the house.

Winchester Mystery House Near San Jose Before the Earthquake

In 1922, after one of these **séances**, Sarah died. She was 83 years old. Legend has it that Sarah's spirit—and the spirits she worked so hard to please—still inhabit the house.

The staircase that leads nowhere in the Winchester Mystery House

INTERESTING FACT

It's said that Sarah slept in a different room each night. Was she trying to confuse her ghostly guests? She also believed spider webs and the number 13 were lucky. Both symbols can be found throughout the house.

In 2005, paranormal investigators Jason Hawes and Grant Wilson traveled to the Winchester House to hunt for ghosts. They started in the basement and soon heard loud, banging sounds. However, Jason and Grant quickly recognized the noises as a plumbing issue. Later, members of their team noticed a **phantom** smell in a ballroom. Jason and Grant believe that ghosts can show up as odd smells. However, after hours of investigating, they weren't able to find concrete evidence of ghosts. "The Winchester Mystery House was certainly mysterious. It's not hard to see why people think it's haunted," said Jason.

Paranormal investigators Jason Hawes and Grant Wilson

Inside the Winchester Mystery House

INTERESTING FACT

Jason and Grant are founders of the Atlantic Paranormal Society (T.A.P.S.) and stars of the TV show *Ghost Hunters*. They say that only 20 percent of their cases turn up paranormal activity.

CHAPTER FOUR

MORRIS-JUMEL MANSION

New York, New York

"Yes indeed, there were and are ghosts at the Morris-Jumel Mansion," said Hans Holzer, who's known as America's first ghost hunter. Built in 1765, the mansion is the oldest house in Manhattan. In 1810, French businessman Stephen Jumel bought the house and lived there with his wife Eliza. Stephen died in 1832 after a mysterious fall, leading some people to think that Eliza had killed him.

The Morris-Jumel House

Eliza remarried U.S. **statesman** Aaron Burr a year later—and divorced him not long after. Eliza quickly became a wealthy businesswoman. She lived in the mansion until her death in 1865. It's said that a restless spirit remains in the house. For decades, people have seen floating objects, heard voices, and have even glimpsed full-body apparitions in the mansion.

INTERESTING FACT

In 1776 during the American Revolution, George Washington used the Morris-Jumel Mansion as his headquarters. The house became a museum in 1903.

In 1964, ghost hunter Hans Holzer investigated the mansion with the help of a **psychic**. Together, they reportedly contacted the spirit of Stephen Jumel. Stephen's spirit claimed that Eliza had killed him—and buried him alive! The medium, however, wasn't able to communicate with Eliza.

The front door of the Morris-Jumel House

That same year, students touring the house spotted a woman screaming on the balcony of the Morris-Jumel Mansion. A museum worker assured them that no one had access to the balcony. The children later saw a portrait of a lady hanging in the house. They were stunned! The person in the painting was Eliza Jumel—the same woman they had seen on the balcony.

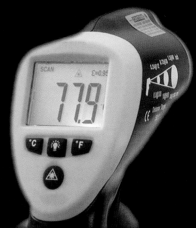

Some ghost hunters use handheld infrared thermometers to detect temperature changes supposedly caused by ghosts.

INTERESTING FACT

In recent years, paranormal investigator Vincent Carbone has used an EMF (electromagnetic field) meter to search for ghostly activity in the mansion. Ghost hunters believe that EMF meters can help determine changes in electromagnetic fields and if a ghost is present. One day inside the house, Vincent asked, "Can you send this light to red please?" The EMF meter changed to red.

Myrtles Plantation

St. Francisville, Louisiana

Surrounded by tall oak trees, the Myrtles Plantation is a 22-room farmhouse that dates to the 1790s. Over the years, different families have lived in the home. Some even died there. Many lost their lives to a disease called yellow fever. One man, William Winter, was shot to death—and, it seems, there's a ghost to prove it.

The Myrtles Plantation

In 1871, William Winter and his family were living at the Myrtles Plantation when a stranger on horseback arrived at the house. He demanded to see William. In an instant, a shot rang out. The stranger had pulled out a gun and fired at William. William collapsed and died soon after.

INTERESTING FACT

There's a famous spooky tale about an enslaved girl named Chloe, who supposedly killed three people at the Myrtles Plantation. So far, experts have been unable to verify the story.

went to the Myrtles to learn about its haunted history. They started their investigation by setting up cameras in and around the house. Something that glowed yellow, indicating heat, moved past one of the thermal cameras. Outside, they noticed a flash in the shape of a human figure. When they reviewed their footage, they found something even more incredible. They saw a lamp slide across a table on its own. "It had moved a good fourteen inches," said Jason. "We couldn't find another explanation," said Jason. "We had to attribute the phenomenon to a **supernatural** force. In other words, the place was haunted." Is William's ghost lingering around the Myrtles Plantation?

Visitors enjoy touring the Myrtles
Plantation's many rooms.

GHOST-HUNTING TOOLS

Here are some basic ghost-hunting tools. Many household items can be used to track and gather evidence of possible ghosts.

- Pen and paper to record your findings
- A flashlight with extra batteries
- A camera with a clean lens. Sometimes, the "**orbs**" that some people capture on film are actually dust particles on the lens.
- A cell phone to use in case of an emergency and to keep track of time
- A camcorder or digital video recorder to capture images of spirits or any other paranormal activity
- A digital audio recorder to capture ghostly sounds or EVPs
- A digital thermometer to pick up temperature changes

More experienced ghost hunters use thermal imaging tools to locate hot and cold spots, as well as special meters to pick up energy fields. These include EMF (electromagnetic field) and RF (radio frequency) meters.

Find Out More

BOOKS

Gardner Walsh, Liza. *Ghost Hunter's Handbook: Supernatural Explorations for Kids*. Lanham, Maryland: Down East Publishing, 2016.

Loh-Hagan, Virginia. *Odd Jobs: Ghost Hunter*. Ann Arbor, Michigan: Cherry Lake Publishing, 2016.

Markovics, Joyce. *Ghastly Gothic Mansions*. New York: Bearport Publishing, 2018.

WEBSITES

American Hauntings
https://www.americanhauntingsink.com

American Paranormal Investigations
https://www.ap-investigations.com

The Atlantic Paranormal Society
http://the-atlantic-paranormal-society.com

Ghost Research Society
http://www.ghostresearch.org

Paranormal Inc.
http://www.paranormalincorporated.com

The Parapsychological Association
https://www.parapsych.org

WORKS CONSULTED

Hawes, Jason, and Grant Wilson. *Ghost Files*. New York: Gallery Books, 2011. New York: Gallery Books, 2011.

Newman, Rich. *Ghost Hunting for Beginners: Everything You Need to Know to Get Started*. Woodbury, Minnesota: Llewellyn Publications, 2018.

Rule, Leslie. *When the Ghost Screams: True Stories of Victims Who Haunt*. Kansas City, Missouri: Andrews McMeel Publishing, 2006.

Taylor, Troy. *The Ghost Hunters Guidebook: The Essential Guide to Investigating Ghosts & Hauntings*. Alton, Illinois: Whitechapel Productions Press, 2004.

Taylor, Troy. *Murdered in Their Beds: History and Hauntings of Villisca and the Midwest Ax Murders*. Alton, Illinois: Whitechapel Productions Press, 2012.

ON THE INTERNET

https://www.americanhauntingsink.com/myrtles

https://www.morrisjumel.org

https://www.myrtlesplantation.com/history-and-hauntings/the-legend-of-chloe

http://nycitylens.com/2019/04/the-oldest-house-in-manhattan-is-rich-with-culture-and-history-and-maybe-even-ghosts/

https://www.psychologytoday.com/us/blog/shadow-boxing/201801/new-york-s-most-haunted-mansion

http://www.villiscaiowa.com

https://www.visitcalifornia.com/attraction/winchester-mystery-house

GLOSSARY

apparition
A ghost or ghostlike image

commune
To feel in close spiritual contact with

devoted
Very loyal

electromagnetic field
A field of energy around a magnetic material or moving electric charge

evidence
Information and facts that help prove something

grisly
Causing horror or disgust

heiress
A female who inherits vast wealth

hive
A place in which there's a lot of activity

medium
A person claiming to communicate between the dead and the living

orbs
Glowing spheres

paranormal
Relating to events not able to be scientifically explained

phantom
Something that is not real and exists only in a person's mind

phenomena
Occurrences that one can sense

psychic
A person claiming to have powers not able to be scientifically explained

pulsing
Throbbing

séances
Meetings in which people try to make contact with the dead

spirits
Supernatural beings such as ghosts

statesman
A skilled, experienced, and respected male political leader

supernatural
Related to a force beyond scientific understanding

thermal
Relating to heat

verify
To prove to be true

Index

About the Author

Matilda Snowden loves all things old and cobwebby and visiting houses with interesting histories. Her favorite thing about being an author is talking with children about how to tell a spooky story.